MW01016095

This book belongs to

_____

Christmas ~
A Holiday Treasury

EDITED BY

Della Rowland

ILLUSTRATED BY

Lynn Bywaters

WITH

Scott Gustafson, Judith Ann Griffith

AND

Jennifer St. Denis

ARIEL BOOKS

ANDREWS AND McMEEL

KANSAS CITY

Library of Congress Catalog Card Number: 93-70496
ISBN: 0-8362-4938-0

Book design by Tony Fradkin

Christmas ~
A Holiday Treasury

The Night Before Christmas

By Clement Clarke Moore

'Twas the night before Christmas, when all
  through the house
Not a creature was stirring, not even a mouse.
The stockings were hung by the chimney with
  care,
In hopes that St. Nicholas soon would be there.

The children were nestled all snug in their beds,
While visions of sugarplums danced in their heads;
And Mama in her kerchief, and I in my cap,
Had just settled our brains for a long winter's nap,
When out on the lawn there arose such a clatter,
I sprang from my bed to see what was the matter.
Away to the window I flew like a flash,
Tore open the shutters and threw up the sash.
The moon on the breast of the new-fallen snow
Gave a luster of midday to objects below;
When what to my wondering eyes should appear
But a miniature sleigh, and eight tiny reindeer,
With a little old driver, so lively and quick,
I knew in a moment it must be Saint Nick!
More rapid than eagles his coursers they came,
And he whistled and shouted and called them
   by name:

"Now, Dasher! Now, Dancer! Now, Prancer and
   Vixen!
On, Comet! On, Cupid! On, Donder and Blitzen!
To the top of the porch! To the top of the wall!
Now dash away! Dash away! Dash away all!"
As dry leaves that before the wild hurricane fly,
When they meet with an obstacle, mount to
   the sky,

So up to the housetop the coursers they flew,
With a sleigh full of toys—and St. Nicholas, too.
And then, in a twinkling, I heard on the roof
The prancing and pawing of each little hoof.
As I drew in my head, and was turning around,
Down the chimney St. Nicholas came with
    a bound.
He was dressed all in fur, from his head to his foot,
And his clothes were all covered with ashes
    and soot;

A bundle of toys he had flung on his back,
And he looked like a peddler just opening
   his pack.
His eyes, how they twinkled! His dimples,
   how merry!
His cheeks were like roses, his nose like a cherry!
His droll little mouth was drawn up like a bow,
And the beard on his chin was as white as
   the snow;
The stump of a pipe he held tight in his teeth,
And the smoke, it encircled his head like a wreath.
He had a broad face and a little round belly
That shook, when he laughed, like a bowlful
   of jelly.
He was chubby and plump, a right jolly old elf,
And I laughed when I saw him, in spite of myself.
A wink of his eye and a twist of his head,
Soon gave me to know I had nothing to dread.

He spoke not a word, but went straight to
   his work,
And filled all the stockings; then turned with
   a jerk,
And laying a finger aside of his nose
And giving a nod, up the chimney he rose.
He sprang to his sleigh, to his team gave a whistle,
And away they all flew like the down of a thistle,
But I heard him exclaim, ere he drove out of sight,
"Happy Christmas to all, and to all a good night!"

O Christmas Tree

TRADITIONAL

O Christmas tree, O Christmas tree!
  How lovely are thy branches!
O Christmas tree, O Christmas tree!
  How lovely are thy branches!
Not only green in summer's heat,
  But also winter's snow and sleet.
O Christmas tree, O Christmas tree!
  How lovely are thy branches!

O Christmas tree, O Christmas tree!
  Thy candles shine out brightly!
O Christmas tree, O Christmas tree!
  Thy candles shine out brightly!
Each bough does hold its tiny light
  That makes each toy to sparkle bright.
O Christmas tree, O Christmas tree!
  Thy candles shine out brightly!

Good King Wenceslas

RETOLD BY DELLA ROWLAND

$\mathcal{K}$ing Wenceslas of Bohemia was such a good man, he was made a saint after his death. Here is the story of one of his kind deeds, told in a famous Christmas carol.

The story takes place on December 26, the holiday honoring St. Stephen. King Wenceslas was looking out his palace window, admiring the moon shining down on the deep white snow. At that moment he saw a man with no coat or shoes gathering firewood.

The King called out to his page, "Who is that poor man and where does he live?"

"Sire," the page replied, "he is a peasant who lives at the foot of the mountain near the edge of the forest."

"Fetch meat and wine and wood," cried the good King. "We will take them to him!"

The King and his page set off that very night. They trudged through the steep snow and leaned into the wild wind. After a while the page cried, "Sire, the bitter cold has made me weak! I can go no farther!"

The King turned and said, "Walk in my footsteps and you will not feel the wind."

When the page stepped into the King's footprint he was astonished to find that the ground was warm where his master had walked! The miraculous heat took away the wind's biting sting, and the page was able to continue on.

That night the page came to realize a great lesson: those who give to the needy shall also have everything they need.

O Little Town of Bethlehem

PHILLIP BROOKS

O little town of Bethlehem
How still we see thee lie;
Above thy deep and dreamless sleep
The silent stars go by.
Yet in thy dark streets shineth
The everlasting Light;
The hopes and fears of all the years
Are met in thee tonight.

Deck the Halls

TRADITIONAL

Deck the halls with boughs of holly,
  Fa la la la la, la la la la.
'Tis the season to be jolly,
  Fa la la la la, la la la la.
Don we now our gay apparel,
  Fa la la, la la la, la la la.
Troll the ancient Yuletide carol,
  Fa la la la la, la la la la.

We Wish You a Merry Christmas

TRADITIONAL

We wish you a Merry Christmas,
We wish you a Merry Christmas,
We wish you a Merry Christmas,
  And a Happy New Year!

Jingle Bells

JAMES PIERPONT

Jingle bells, jingle bells,
Jingle all the way!
Oh, what fun it is to ride
In a one-horse open sleigh!
Jingle bells, jingle bells,
Jingle all the way!
Oh, what fun it is to ride
In a one-horse open sleigh!

🌿 *What Can I Give Him?* 🌿

CHRISTINA ROSETTI

*W*hat can I give Him,
   Poor as I am?
If I were a shepherd
   I would bring a lamb,
If I were a wise man
   I would do my part,—
Yet what can I give Him?
   Give my heart.

🌿 *I Heard the Bells on Christmas Day* 🌿

HENRY WADSWORTH LONGFELLOW

I heard the bells on Christmas Day
Their old familiar carols play
And wild and sweet the words repeat
Of peace on earth, good will to men.

The Twelve Days of Christmas

TRADITIONAL ENGLISH CAROL

On the first day of Christmas
My true love sent to me
A partridge in a pear tree.

On the second day of Christmas
My true love sent to me
Two turtle doves
and a partridge in a pear tree.

On the third day of Christmas…
Three French hens, (repeat)

On the fourth day of Christmas…
Four calling birds, (repeat)

On the fifth day of Christmas…
Five gold rings, (repeat)

On the sixth day of Christmas...
Six geese a-laying, (repeat)

On the seventh day of Christmas...
Seven swans a-swimming, (repeat)

On the eighth day of Christmas...
Eight maids a-milking, (repeat)

On the ninth day of Christmas...
Nine drummers drumming, (repeat)

On the tenth day of Christmas...
Ten pipers piping, (repeat)

On the eleventh day of Christmas...
Eleven ladies dancing, (repeat)

On the twelfth day of Christmas...
Twelve lords a-leaping, (repeat)

❦ *Patapan* ❦

*W*illie, take your little drum,
   With your whistle, Robin, come!
When we hear the fife and drum
   Ture-lure-lu, pata-pata-pan,
When we hear the fife and drum
   Christmas should be frolicsome.

Santa Claus

ANONYMOUS

He comes in the night!
He comes in the night!
He softly, silently comes;
While the little brown heads
  on the pillows so white
Are dreaming of bugles and drums.
He cuts through the snow
  like a ship through the foam,
While the white flakes around him whirl;
Who tells him I know not,
  but he findeth the home
Of each good little boy and girl.

Here We Come A-Caroling

TRADITIONAL

Here we come a-caroling
  Among the leaves so green;
Here we come a-wand'ring
  So fair to be seen.

God bless the master of the house
  Likewise the mistress, too;
And all the little children
  That round the table go.

Love and joy come to you
  And a joyful Christmas, too,
And God bless you and send
  You a Happy New Year—
And God send you a Happy New Year.

The Visit of the Three Wise Men

RETOLD BY DELLA ROWLAND

$\mathcal{J}$ust before Jesus' birth, three wise men saw a strange star in the sky and heard a voice say, "Today a King is born in Judea."

Loading their camels with gifts, these wise men set out for Jerusalem, where Herod, the king of Judea, lived. "Where is the baby who will become the King?" they asked Herod.

"My priests say he is in Bethlehem," King Herod told the wise men. "When you find him, come and tell me where he is so I can worship him, too." But secretly Herod planned to kill the child, for he was afraid he would lose his throne to this baby.

As the wise men started out for Bethlehem, the star appeared again to guide them. At last, it stopped and shone a great light on a small, poor house. Inside were Mary and Joseph and baby Jesus. When the wise men saw that the star's light shone around Jesus, they fell to their knees, and offered him gold, myrrh, and frankincense.

That night, an angel warned them of Herod's evil plan, so they left Bethlehem, taking a different route home. On a sacred hill, they built a shrine to Jesus and agreed to meet there once a year. Then, full of joy, they went home, telling everyone they met of the newborn king they had seen.

Christmas Eve

WASHINGTON IRVING

*N*ow Christmas is come,
  Let us beat up the drum,
And call our neighbors together,
  And when they appear,
  Let us make them such cheer,
As will keep out the wind and the weather.

The Holly and the Ivy

TRADITIONAL

The holly and the ivy
Now both are full-well grown,
Of all the trees that are in the wood
The holly bears the crown.
Oh, the rising of the sun
And the running of the deer,
The playing of the merry organ,
Sweet singing in the choir!

Little Jack Horner

Little Jack Horner sat in the corner
Eating his Christmas pie.
He put in his thumb,
and pulled out a plum,
And said, "What a good boy am I!"

How the Nutcracker Defeated the Mouse King

RETOLD BY DELLA ROWLAND

$\mathcal{I}$t was past bedtime on Christmas Eve—and time for Marie to put away her new Nutcracker. She had just closed the door to the toy cabinet when, *poom*, the clock struck midnight. At that instant, hundreds of mice began squeezing through the cracks in the wall! Squeaking and squealing, they lined up in neat little rows like troops of soldiers.

Then, with a loud CRACK! the floor opened up. Out burst a mouse with seven heads and seven gold crowns, and each head was hissing frightfully. To Marie's horror, it ordered the mouse army to attack the toys!

Inside the cabinet a voice shouted, *"Knack knack, the mousey pack, their skulls we'll crack, a cowardly pack."* It was the Nutcracker! And the toys joined in reply, *"Awake and fight for what is right! Up now, away —this is the night!"*

The Nutcracker waved his sword in the air.
With flags flying and drums rolling, the toys
jumped out of the cabinet and lined up behind
him! *Boom! Boom!* the toy cannons blasted the
mice army with sugarplums and walnuts. The
mice soldiers in turn filled their guns with silver
sprinkles from Christmas cookies and fired at the
glass doors of the toy cabinet.

Through the powdered sugar smoke Marie
could see the toys battling bravely, but they were
no match for the mice. The china dolls were so

stiff and slow, they were shattered in no time. It was quite easy for the mice to bite off the gingerbread people's legs. The plush animals were badly chewed up, too, and could barely move, having lost most of their stuffing. Only the tin soldiers were holding their own but they were badly outnumbered.

The Nutcracker lost his sword and was seized by two mice soldiers. The Mouse King scurried toward him, all seven heads squeaking in triumph. At that, Marie pulled off her shoe and hurled it at the Mouse King!

The battle stopped as the mouse general fell to the floor. Quickly the Nutcracker grabbed his sword and ran the Mouse King through! With an awful *hiss-ssss* the horrible creature died.

Instantly, the mice army vanished, and all the toys were sitting in the toy cabinet. The Nutcracker kneeled before Marie. "With your help," he said, "I have killed the Mouse King. Now will you help me break the spell his mother, Dame Mouserink, put on me?"

Because Marie loved her Nutcracker, she agreed. But that, dear reader, is another story!